Leabharlanna Poibli Chathair Baile Átha Cliath

Dublin City Public Libraries

Bear LOVES fishing!

Emily Gravett

Bear and Hare

Go Fishing

MACMILLAN CHILDREN'S BOOKS

Bear and Hare are going fishing.

Bear fished. He fished . . .

Hare's hat.

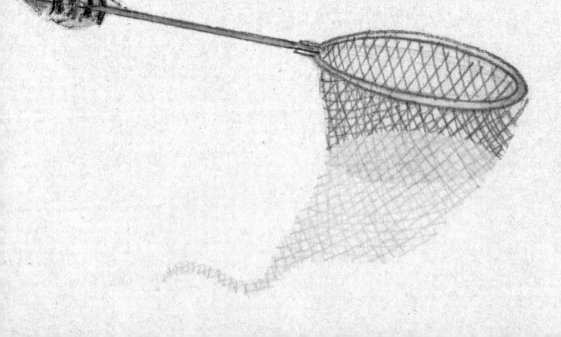

He fished . . .

a frog!

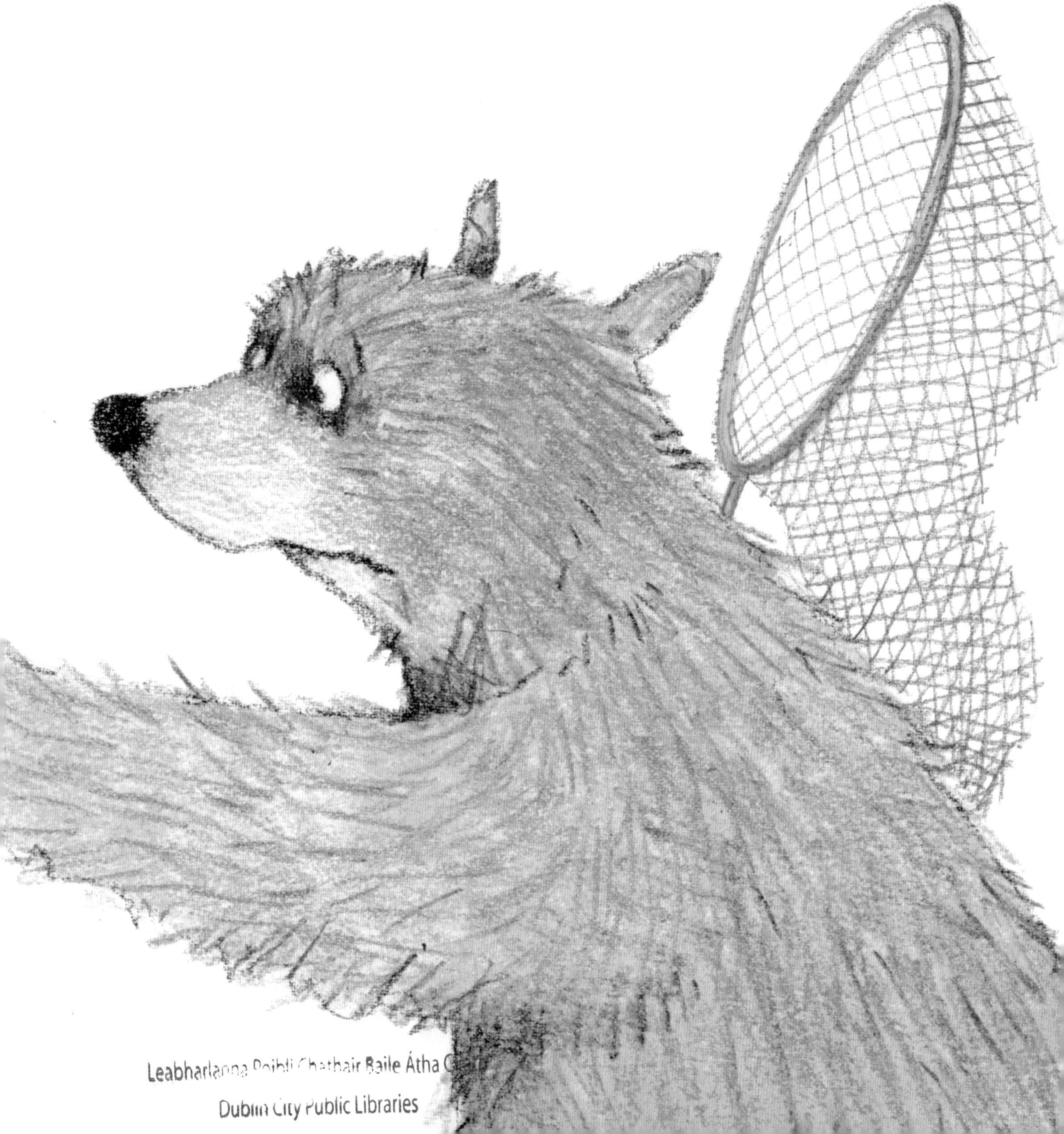

He fished . . .

a rollerskate.

Bear fished.

He fished . . .

And fished . . .

And . . .

fished!

For Cecily & Laily

First published 2014 by Macmillan Children's Books, a division of Macmillan Publishers Limited, 20 New Wharf Road, London N1 9RR, Basingstoke and Oxford Associated companies throughout the world. www.panmacmillan.com ISBN: 978-0-230-74539-1 Text and illustrations copyright © Emily Gravett 2014. Moral rights asserted. Printed in China

1 3 5 7 9 8 6 4 2 A CIP catalogue record for this book is available from the British Library.